TO ADITYA

MAC

W9-DJM-402

KHALA MANINGE
The little elephant that cried a lot
AN AFRICAN FABLE

To Milo and Faren

Written by Ian C. MacMillan
Illustrated by Eric G. MacMillan

Published by

ManingeMali Publishing
204 Garden Place
Radnor PA 19087
USA

e-mail: ManingeMali@AOL.COM

To order a copy of this book, see the last page.

Khala Maninge* (KAH-lah mah-NING-ghe) was crying again. She was such a sad little elephant, so unhappy. She thought nobody liked her. All the other baby animals teased her about her long funny nose, and her big flappy ears, and her stumpy legs with their little flat feet.

She was so sad and always crying, so this is how she got her name—Khala Maninge means "Cries a Lot" in Zulu.

Today she had decided to get away from the teasing animals by heading off into the bush to be by herself.

She was leaning up against a big ugly tree crying to herself, wishing and wishing that she could be pretty so that everyone would admire her. Suddenly a deep voice asked, "Why are you crying little elephant?"

She looked around in fright and saw nobody and shouted: "Where are you?" And the deep voice said, "You're leaning on me. I am the Magic Baobab tree—I can talk. Why are you so unhappy?"

So Khala told the Magic Baobab how the animals teased her because she was ugly, and how she wished she could be pretty and admired by all.

The Baobab tree said, "Let me tell you a story about what happened to me long, long ago."

* African names have been simplified. Approximate pronunciation can be seen at the back of the book.

Khala and the Magic Baobab

The Magic Baobab said: "As you can see I am a very ugly tree - I have a huge fat pinky-blue trunk with tiny little branches and silly little leaves on top. All the other trees mocked me for being ugly, so I also cried and cried like you."

"Then early one morning Khova Sangoma Enkulu (which means 'The Great Owl Wizard' in Xhosa) flew onto my branches, to rest from his night of hunting."

"When he heard me crying he asked me why. So I told him how unhappy I was about being teased, and how I wished I could be admired and respected by others."

"Khova said: 'You can earn your own respect and happiness, but you must work at it. Instead of spending your time crying about what others say about you, spend that time thinking about how to advise others who are unhappy. If you help others by giving them good advice, they will respect you, and with respect comes your self-made happiness.' "

"Then Khova cast a spell which gave me a voice to speak to others and give them advice. Now instead of worrying about myself, I think only about advising others who are unhappy."

"Over the years many animals have come upon me, just like you have, and often I have been able to give them advice. Now I have the respect of all who know of me."

"Then I will do the same," said Khala Maninge.

"Don't think it is easy," said the Magic Baobab. "You may have to think very hard to come up with good advice."

Khova the Great Owl Wizard

But Khala rushed off, eager to give advice to all and sundry.

The first person she met was a little girl giraffe called Xale Njamala bou Djiguene (a seriously big name for a little girl! It means "Little Girl Giraffe" in Wolof). Njamala was looking very unhappy about herself. "What's the matter?" asked Khala Maninge.

"I'm so tall and so gawky with a long skinny neck and long skinny legs and as I get older I will just get taller and ganglier and sillier looking," cried Njamala.

"Then what you should do is kneel down so you won't look tall," said Khala Maninge.

"That is the silliest advice I have ever heard," said Njamala. "If I did that I wouldn't be able to walk or eat!"

"Go away you silly elephant!" shouted the giraffe.

So Khala slunk off, feeling as unhappy as ever.

But then Khala thought about what had gone wrong and she said to herself: "It did not help advising Njamala to pretend she was not tall."

"Maybe the right way to help others is to help them see what is good about themselves, so they stop worrying about what they don't like about themselves."

"I will try that the next time I give advice to anyone."

Khala Maninge and Njamala the Giraffe

The next day she came upon Kiboko Kisichana ("Little Girl Hippo" in Swahili), who was looking very sorry for herself.

"I am so fat and so ugly and as I get older I will just get fatter," wailed Kiboko.

"Let me think about this," said Khala Maninge to herself, because Kiboko really was pretty porky! So she thought and she thought about all the things that hippos do.

"I've got it!" said Khala Maninge. "You hippos get fat because you eat up all the river weeds! But if you didn't eat them, the weeds would grow and grow and clog the whole river. Then the river would dam up and flood the countryside and drown the animals."

"So-oh............the more weeds you eat, and the fatter you get, the better!"

"Let's hang a sign on you that says in big letters: I EAT TO SAVE YOU FROM DROWNING and everyone will know that the fatter you are, the better for them!"

When they did this Kiboko was so happy and proud of her plump little rump that she waddled it to show it off as she walked away. And that is why Hippos waddle when they walk.

Kiboko the little hippo girl – ready to waddle

Next Khala Maninge met a very sad baboon called Gudo Chijaya ("Boy Baboon" in Shona) who was mega-upset.

"I look SERIOUSLY goofy," cried Gudo. "It's bad enough that I have a big red bottom on my back end, but I also have two tiny beady little eyes stuck close together at my front end. I look like TOTALLY uncool!"

And Gudo wasn't kidding about looking goofy with his small, close-set eyes, but Khala Maninge thought and thought and thought about what baboons do.

Then Khala got it! She laughed excitedly and said: "You are always picking at things with your inquisitive little hands. You can use your sharp eyes and your clever little hands to remove thorns from the paws of the other animals before their paws get infected!"

"So-o-oh.........the smaller your eyes, and the closer they are together, the better you can see the thorns!"

"Let's hang a sign around your neck that says: MY EYES ARE SMALL AND CLOSE TOGETHER SO I CAN SEE THE THORNS I PULL OUT."

And Gudo was so happy he did a somersault of joy, then ran off proudly showing everyone his sign, and that is how Baboons learned to do somersaults.

Gudo the beady-eyed baboon

The next animal Khala Maninge met was a very unhappy little boy Hyena. He was called Yaro Siyaki (Hausa for "Boy Hyena"), and was he ever depressed!

"I am hated by EVERYONE," complained Siyaki. "They hate my ugliness. They hate my weird way of walking with my short back and my long front legs. But they hate me most of all because of my huge strong jaws that I will use to crunch up their bones when they die."

"Wow!" thought Khala Maninge. "This guy Siyaki is PLENTY ugly and mean looking! Is this going to be a tough job of advising or what?"

But she thought and she thought, and she thought and she thought, and then she thought some more.

"Wait a minute!" she said: "If you don't eat the bones of the animals when they die, their bodies will cause disease! By eating the bones you are saving all the animals from terrible diseases."

"So-o-o-oh.........the stronger your jaws are the better!"

"Let's put a huge sign around your neck that says: MY STRONG JAWS SAVE YOU FROM DISEASE."

And Siyaki was so happy that as he loped off wearing his new sign, he began to laugh and laugh and laugh.

And that is how Hyenas learned to laugh.

Siyaki the hyena boy laughed and laughed

Khala Maninge was very happy that she had helped Kiboko and Gudo and Siyaki, but it still bothered her that she had not helped Njamala.

She kept on fretting about the silly advice she had given to the girl giraffe – telling her to try to hide her long neck and legs by kneeling down.

"What use are a long neck and long legs?" she wondered.

Suddenly Khala Maninge had a great idea!

She rushed back to Njamala and she said: "With your long neck only you can look over the tops of the trees for the smoke from bush fires."

"When you see the smoke of the coming fires and begin to run, this warns all the other animals that there is a fire coming."

"The taller that you are, the higher are the trees that you will be able to see over to spot the fires coming."

"So-o-o-o-oh.........the longer your legs and neck are the better!"

"Let's put a humongous sign on your neck saying: MY LONG NECK SAVES YOU FROM THE BUSH FIRES."

Njamala was so excited at the idea that she squeaked with joy, and she squeaked so hard that she lost her voice.

And that is why Giraffes have no voice.

Njamala feeling pret-ty tall

As the years went by, everyone in the bush learned to come to Khala Maninge for advice.

She became wiser and wiser and gained more and more respect.

As she helped others, she became happier and more confident, but it was because she had earned her own happiness and confidence by herself, and didn't depend on others for it.

And then one day she woke up and found all the animals gathered around her with a super-humongous jy-normous sign that said: WE LOVE YOU INDLOVU INTWESI (which means "Wise Elephant" in Zulu).

"Thank you, thank you, Magic Baobab," whispered Indlovu Intwesi to herself.

And miles and miles away the Magic Baobab Tree heard the silent whisper and smiled to himself.

And that is how the Elephant became the wisest of the animals.

(And also why Elephants never push Baobab trees over, no matter how hungry they are.)

Khala becomes Indlovu Intwesi

Pronouncing the African names

Below, the emphasis is indicated by capitalized syllables and the approximate pronunciation is as follows:

-ah is pronounced as in far
-aw is pronounced as in paw
-e   is pronounced as in bet
-ee is pronounced as in bee
gh- is pronounced as in God
-i   is pronounced as in fig
-oe is pronounced as in toe
-oo is pronounced as in zoo

So-o-o-oh......

Khala Maninge	KAH-lah mah-NING-ghe
Khova Sangoma Enkulu	KAW-vah sahn-GAW-mah en-KOO-loo
Xale Njamala bou Djiguene	KAH-le nn-jah-MAH-lah BOO jee-GWEN-e
Kiboko Kisichana	ki-BAW-kaw ki-si-CHAH-nah
Gudo Chijaya	GOO-daw chi-JAH-yah
Yaro Siyaki	YAH-roe si-YAH-ki
Indlovu Intwesi	in-DLAW-voo in-TWE-si

Locations of the African Languages

Zulu and Xhosa are the languages of the Zulu and the Xhosa people in South Africa. (Milo and Faren's mother spent many years in South Africa.)

Wolof is a language spoken mostly by people in Senegal in West Africa. (Milo and Faren's family friend Bineta comes from Senegal.)

Swahili is a language spoken all over East Africa. (Milo and Faren's great-grandmother was born in Kenya in East Africa.)

Hausa is a language spoken by many people in the North of Sub-Saharan Africa. (Milo and Faren's great-grandfather worked in Nigeria where Hausa is one of many languages spoken.)

Shona is a language spoken by many people in Central Africa. (Milo and Faren's granddad lived in Central Africa where Shona is one of many languages spoken.)

To order copies of this book:

If you are a school, library or not-for-profit:
Copy this page and mail it to the address below, and we will send you one free book. The charge is five US dollars for each additional book.

If you are NOT a school, library or not-for-profit:
Copy this page and mail it to the address below with a money order for five US dollars per book.

For all orders from outside the USA:
Include an additional two US dollars per book to cover the cost of airmail postage expenses.

If you have questions regarding your order:
E-mail us at ManingeMali@AOL.COM

Name:_____

Organization (if not-for-profit):_____

Address:_____

_____

_____

Number of copies:_____

Mail with money order enclosed to:
ManingeMali Publishers
204 Garden Place
Radnor PA 19087
USA